A Flat             "DUMPTY'S DEFINITIONS"

First U.S. Edition

First published in Great Britain in 1995 by William Heinemann Ltd., an imprint of Reed Consumer Books Ltd., Michelin House, 81 Fulham Road, London SW3 6RB, and Auckland, Melbourne, Singapore, and Toronto

ISBN: 0-316-60202-7
Library of Congress Catalog Card Number 95-75601

1 0 9 8 7 6 5 4 3 2 1

Consulting Designer: Douglas Martin     Paper Engineer: David Hawcock
Produced by Mandarin Offset     Printed and bound in Singapore

# FOR YOU

Once upon a summer's morning,
The Jolly Postman woke up yawning,
Cooked his breakfast, fed the dog,
Read the paper, kissed the frog,*

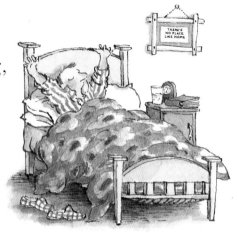

Got his coat and grabbed his hat,
Found his tire was pancake flat,
"Blow me down!" (Blow me up!),
Went back for another cup,

Rubbed his chin, scratched his head . . .
And *walked* to work instead.

*Only joking

A letter for the miller,
A postcard for the mice,
A parcel for the pussycat,
A pair of boots—that's nice!
A letter for a long-haired girl
A letter for a shoe!
A phone bill for a rowboat,
But, goodness—where's the crew?

The Jolly Postman takes his ease,
A shady spot, a cool breeze.
Till, suddenly—Oh, dear! Oh, my!—
A *giant rattle* from the sky
Gives him a tremendous clout . . .
And knocks him out.

Meanwhile, above, a giant mother
Says, "Never mind, we'll buy another."

The tire was flat, the Postman's flatter;
His poor dog wonders what's the matter.
He licks his master's pale cheek.
The Postman seems about to speak.
"I'll be all right—I'm feeling better."
And then a rabbit with a *letter*
Goes running by; the dog gives chase.
The Postman, too, joins in the race.
All three of them—well, bless my soul—
Go diving down a rabbit hole.

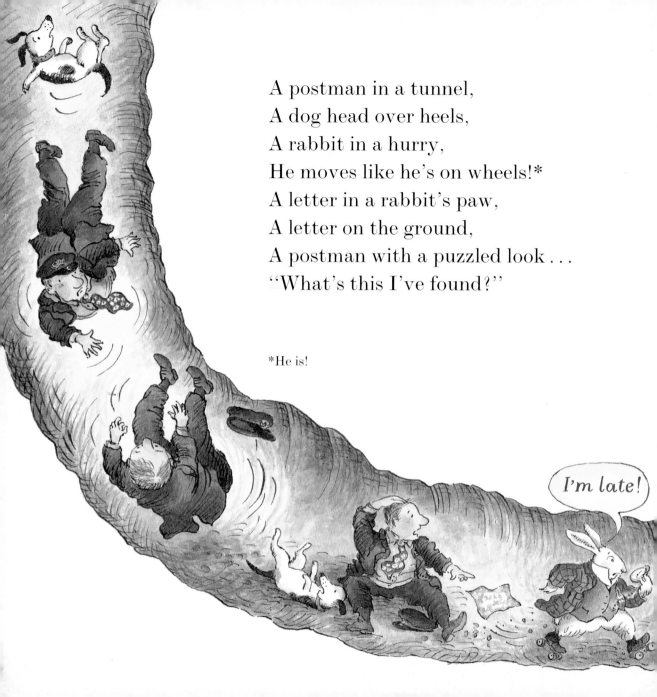

A postman in a tunnel,
A dog head over heels,
A rabbit in a hurry,
He moves like he's on wheels!*
A letter in a rabbit's paw,
A letter on the ground,
A postman with a puzzled look . . .
"What's this I've found?"

*He is!

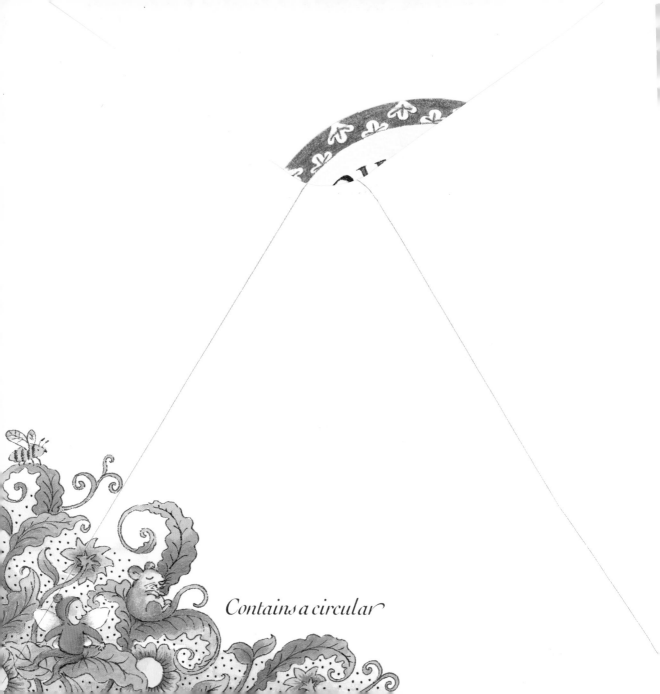

*Contains a circular*

And now—hurray!—the Postman sees
A table set beneath the trees,
A girl (named Alice) in a chair,
A Hatter and a Mad March Hare.
"Good-bye! Hello there! Lovely weather!"
The Hare and Hatter shout together.
While Alice says, "Here, sit by me.
How are you? Would you like some tea?"

The Postman sips, the Postman drinks.
    The Postman shivers . . . smiles
         . . . and *shrinks.*

         What will he do?
         How will he cope?
          He's shut up
           Like a
            tele-
            scope!*

       *And his dog, too.

"My word!" the Pocket Postman cries,
Astonished by his pocket size,
His pocket dog, his pocket hat.
"What kind of cup of tea was that?"

With tiny steps in tiny shoes,
He travels on in search of clues
And finds, quite soon, a curious tree
Of letters. "Is there one for me?"

Alice, meanwhile, now twelve feet tall,
Has made a face
                and begun to bawl.
She ate the little EAT ME cake:
A *huge* mistake.

# Postman

INSURE AGAINST ACCIDENTS

HOBGOBLIN INDEMNITY COMPANY

A flabbergasted postman,
A scary spidergram,
A postman in a pickle,
A postman in a jam.
But now, look out,
There's worse to come.
Don't stop—Keep going—
Scram!

A bat, a rat, three newts, a frog
Pursue the Postman and his dog.
"Is this a dream or am I mad?"
Then, just when things look *really* bad,
The Postman's cries for help are heard
By a friendly passing *postal* bird.

TO ESCAPE
THE HORDE
CLIMB ABOARD

MAIL

Feeling better, flying high,
The Postman waves the bat bye-bye,
Thanks the pilot—"First-class flight!"—
Bails out at a dizzy height,
And lands with a bump on a cookie tin.
"Is anyone in?"

Meanwhile, a *wolf* in postman's clothes
(How did he get them? Goodness knows.)
Arrives to offer bad advice.
(Shut your eyes, this part's not nice.)
"EAT ME? DRINK ME?—that won't do.
This'll solve it: I'll eat you!"

"No fear!" the Postman cries. "You scamp!"
And climbs into the nearest . . . stamp.

WONDERFUL · COPENHAGEN ·

Jolly
The (Visitor
McVitie House
Little Toe Lane
TOYTOWN

Away from the house and down the lane,
The Peppered Postman racks his brain.
As he worries more about being less,
He meets a girl in a gingham dress,
A scarecrow, a lion and a tall tin man,
Who offer to help him all they can.
"You must come with us," they cry, "because . . .
WE'RE OFF TO SEE THE WIZARD OF OZ!"

Then, just when the Postman's about to agree,
He's blown away by sneeze number three.

ATISHOO!

Blow me down! Blow my nose!
Man in daisy; dog in rose.
Meanwhile, above them in the sky,
A *flying* letter flutters by.
Without a name and no address;
For whom is it intended? Guess.

# AIR MAIL

POSTAGE PAID

**2**

SUNNY SIDE
OF STREET

A postman with a sparkling map;
A girl (named Dorothy).
"This is the place we told you of—
The road to Oz!" says she.

A postman with a tiny frown;
A tiny dog, so small,
You almost need a microscope*
To know he's there at all.

*Or a lens

Meanwhile, a girl
so hugely high
You'd need a *telescope*
to spy
If she had washed
her neck or ears,
Above the "tiny" trees
appears.*

"It's only me,
for goodness sake;
All I did was eat a
cake.
Then I shot up like
a rocket!"
She has the Hatter
in her pocket.

*Alice, of course

And now—almost—the final scene:
Down in the clover, cool and green,
The puzzled Postman rubs his chin
And wonders, "How did this begin?"
Suddenly—Oh, dear! Oh, my!—
The *Gingerbread Boy* comes hurtling by;
Avoids with ease the Hatter's hat,
But knocks the Jolly Postman . . . *FLAT.*

A curious rippling in the air,
A ringing in the ears.
The scene begins to shift and fade
Until . . . it disappears.

A postman, much to his surprise,
Returned now to his former size.
Things are not always what they seem.
Was all that shrinking just a dream?

A miller with a cup of tea.
"You've had a nasty bump," says he.

Once upon a summer's morning,
The Jolly Postman wakes up yawning,
With a bandage round his head
And a crowd around his bed,
And a dog curled up upon it,
And a baby in a bonnet;
A bottle and a spoon:
Three times daily—get well soon.

And the nurse says, "Feeling better?
Look, the postman's brought a letter!"*

*Post*woman*, actually

SOMEWHERE OVER THE RAINBOW

EMERALD CITY
COUNCIL

10 OZ

5 OZ

TO The Jolly Postman
Wincey Ward
Cock Robin Memorial
Hospital

The Jolly Postman reads his book
With, once more, a puzzled look,
Eats his breakfast on a tray,
Gets up later in the day,
Takes his medicine, takes a stroll,
Sees a gander score a goal,*
Eats his supper—cheese and bread—
Reads his book again in bed,
Snuggles down—a cozy spot—
And starts to dream . . . or maybe not.

*_Not_ joking!

Meanwhile, from a tremendous height,
Out in the dark and starry night,
Above the hills and under the sky,
Where warm winds blow and witches fly,
Head over heels and golden brown,
A giant . . . *teddy* tumbles down.

The End (really)